KINSLEY ELITE
Series

Colton's Secret: A Prequel
Colton's Legacy: Book One

Colton's
SECRET

USA TODAY BESTSELLING AUTHOR
A.C. KRAMER

Colton's Secret
Copyright © 2021 A.C. Kramer

Editing by: Outthink Editing, LLC
Proofreading by: Jean Bachen & Katie Schmahl
Interior Formatting by: Murphy Wallace
Cover Photography: CJC Photography
Cover Models: Dominic Calvani & Victoria Benavides
Cover Design by: Emma Rider, Moonstruck Cover Design

Print Edition
ISBN: 978-1-954183-59-9

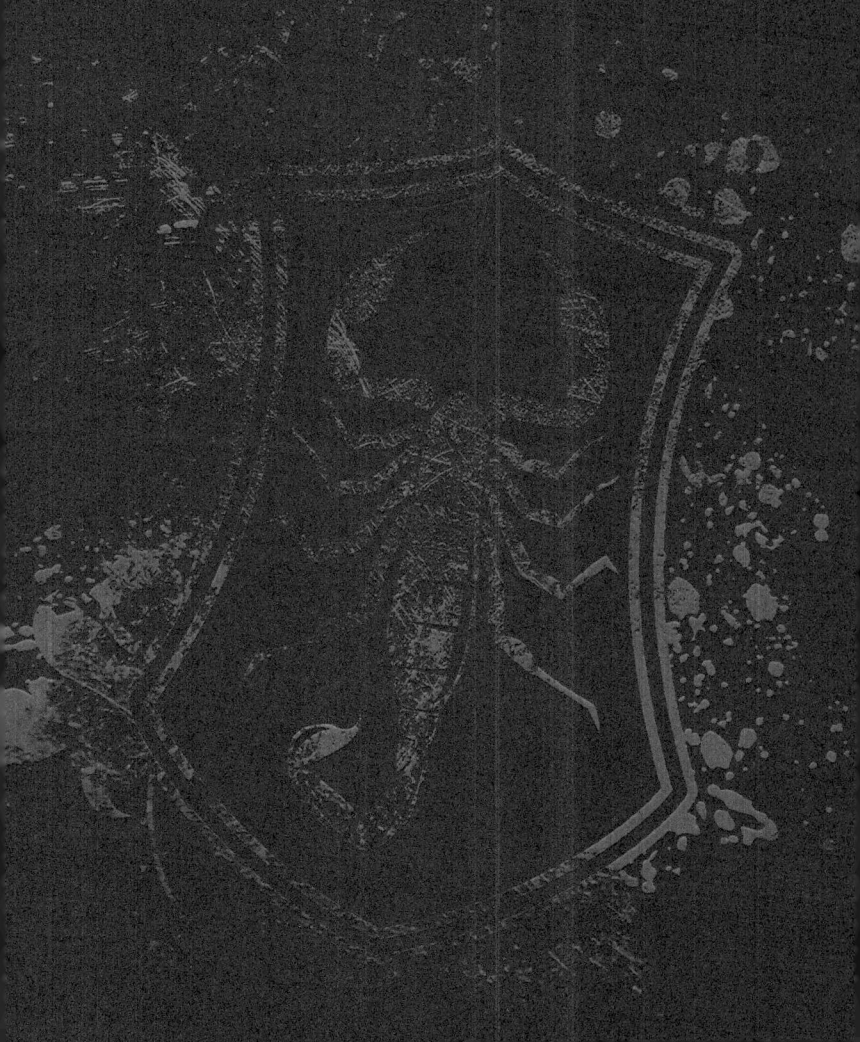

To the voices that followed me with each stroke, bolstered each kick, and encouraged me to achieve my dreams…

Dear Reader,

I've always been a dreamer. Stories and voices live in my head every moment of every day, but there's always been one place where they are louder—in the water.

Swimming is my favorite form of exercise. It also serves as a safe place to daydream and think through plots.

So when I was invited into The Elites boxset, I decided to do something a little different. I mingled my love of a beautiful sport with the darkness of the Scorpio Society world. This is the result of that dangerous twist.

The Kinsley Elite isn't for the faint of heart. There will be dark undertones, cruel games, and harsh moments. Colton's Secret is only the beginning, and while it may read lighter for now, I promise it'll grow in intensity and darkness as the story moves on.

I hope you enjoy Colton and Emma's story.

But prepare yourselves; it's going to be a long swim.

Hugs,
A.C. Kramer

Colton's
SECRET

A Kinsley Elite Prequel

Not all dreams have a happy ending.
A truth I learned the hard way.
All thanks to Colton Kinsley.

When Stonewall University offered me a
full-ride scholarship and a coveted spot in
their esteemed swimming program, it was an
immediate yes. Why?

Because of Colton Kinsley.
Swimming god.
A legend.
The ultimate idol.

It didn't matter that he'd since graduated from
the program. He was still training in the same
pool, preparing for next year's Olympic Games.
And I intended to go with him.
But his family had other plans for me.

My first day of winter semester practice ended
in a nightmare. A pledge. A future I had no
desire to entertain. And Colton Kinsley became
so much more than a mere idol. He became my
mentor for the Scorpio Society.

Now there's no escape.
No alternatives.
No way out.
This is the world of the elite.
To remain, I must obey.
To live, I need to win.

Suit up. It's going to be a long swim.

PROLOGUE

Colton

Water provides me with freedom. Peace. A brief tranquility for my darkening soul.

I count my strokes.

Even my breaths.

Flip perfectly at each wall.

Kick.

Start again.

My coach is timing me. My former teammates are watching me. My ancestors are cursing me.

Every perfect stroke. Every strong kick. Every rhythmic inhale. I'm haunted. Hunted. Claimed and owned.

I never had a choice.

The Scorpio Society possessed me at birth, proclaiming me as one of them. The son of an Elder. An Elite by blood.

I live and breathe this world. All my actions are controlled by those I report to, and dictated by the Elders.

My father has chosen a new recruit.

An Olympic hopeful.

Female.

A freshman. Full-ride scholarship to Stonewall University. My new charge.

It's my job to mold her. Push her. And eventually induct her. But only if she follows every rule and accomplishes all the tasks set out before her.

It won't be easy.

Nothing with the Scorpio Society ever is.

She's off to a decent start, breaking a handful of university records in last week's winter invitational. Although, she'll need to do a lot better if she wants to survive her initiation.

Poor girl has no idea what's coming for her. She just knows she's a recruit. A Scorpio Society hopeful. But no one has explained what that requires yet.

However, she'll understand soon. Just as soon as I reach this wall.

I allow the water to wash it all away for three more strokes. No breaths. One final kick. Then I touch the wall and stand.

Emma Adrian's initiation starts tonight.

CHAPTER ONE

Emma

Colton Kinsley is a god.

The way he moves through the water leaves me hypnotized on the deck, my mind temporarily lost to his long, lean form as he cuts through the pool with expert ease.

It's like a dream.

I've waited for this moment for months. He's the reason I accepted Stonewall University's full-ride scholarship. I've longed to train with him, to learn from him, to study his technique. But he spent last semester in Arizona, training with Coach Rogers.

I understood the choice. Lincoln Rogers's swimming programs were famous, and positions within them were highly coveted. He only accepted the best of the best.

Which Colton clearly qualifies as with his five gold medals, two silver medals, and solo bronze.

One day, I'm going to join him in the elite circle.

Six months, I tell myself, winding my arms in a circle, loosening myself up for practice.

Everyone else is still ogling the god in the pool. Coach Hawkins stands on the deck, admiring Colton's kick as he pushes off a wall. I pity the men's team today—they're all going to be compared to Stonewall University's living swim legend.

As a female, I'm exempt.

But I'll accept the challenge anyway and prove that I'm worthy of sharing this pool with the likes of Colton Kinsley.

I bend to touch my palms to the ground, wiggling my hips around to loosen them up from my earlier jog. My academic advisor scheduled one of my classes clear across the university grounds, with an end time of twenty minutes prior to practice. When I asked her about it, she said there were no alternatives.

So jogging is my new daily dry-land activity.

And I loathe it.

Standing upright once more, I catch Lanie's gaze. She's grinning from ear to ear, excitement radiating from her like sunshine on an August day in Georgia.

She'll be the first to introduce herself to Colton.

And she'll ensure all her assets are on proper display.

The girl has a mean breaststroke in the pool, marking her as a rival of mine in the two hundred individual medley. Because breaststroke is so not my jam. Butterfly, absolutely. Backstroke, not bad. But breaststroke is where I lose it every time.

However, Lanie swims to keep up her physique and to enjoy the male attention that physique acquires.

Which makes her easy to beat in a race.

Because I'm here to win. To be the best. To achieve a childhood dream. To become an Olympian.

Squatting down, I dip my cap into the water to wet the silicon before pulling it over my thick hair. Even in a ponytail, the dark strands reach my lower back—not the most ideal for a swimmer. But neither are my curves. Fortunately, I've learned to work with what God gave me. My hips add to my butterfly kick. The bulge in my cap is great for holding on to my goggles when diving off the starting block. And my breasts, well, the swimsuit compresses those unhelpful bits into a streamlined shape.

Perfection.

Or as close as I can be to it, anyway.

I glance at the board—the one all my teammates are ignoring in favor of Colton—and decipher Coach Hawkins's handwriting. It takes a few seconds for me to translate, but I follow in the end. With a nod, I jump into the pool, taking over the lane beside the god just as he executes a flawless flip turn.

Several of my teammates murmur in surprise.

I grin.

"Warm-up's on the board, y'all," I tell them, gesturing to Coach's infamously bad scrawl. He's old-school and uses chalk, too. Just thinking about touching the board gives me hives.

With a shiver, I push off the wall and start into my warm-up.

Colton pauses at the next wall in the deeper section of the pool. His long legs kick to keep his six-foot-four frame above water, and I flip in the lane beside him, pretending not to notice.

Oh, but I feel his eyes on me.

I've disturbed his peace.

He had a ten-lane pool all to himself, and I ruined his fun by taking over my lane.

Well, practice started five minutes ago. And a proper gentleman would appreciate the need to share.

From what I know about Colton, he's kind, intelligent, and notoriously shy around the cameras. His father is Clive Kinsley—the CEO of Kinsley Associates, a famous law firm known for taking on the world's most elite clientele.

Which means Colton has rubbed elbows with celebrities and their children all his life.

And he knows how to avoid the cameras and reporters.

Not that swimmers gain a lot of notoriety. Our sport tends to only be reported on every four years during the Olympics.

I flip at the opposite end, then start my way down the twenty-five-yard pool once more. This training pool is meant for the winter season. I prefer the fifty-meter one next door since that's the proper Olympic size. But the championships in a few months will be in yards, not meters.

After several more laps—and with Colton treading water in the deep end the whole time—my teammates start to join me. Jesi is first, taking a place in my lane because we like to train together. Lanie joins us, too.

And by the time we've finished warm-ups, Colton has left the pool. He's nowhere to be seen, suggesting he escaped into the locker room.

Coach acts like Colton was never here as he barks out instructions for our two-hour practice.

It's distance day, so the sets are long and arduous. When we're done, my arms and legs feel like Jell-O. I'm eternally grateful when Coach gives us the warm-down set, putting us only about ten minutes over time. Considering our late start, I'm not surprised.

"Ugh, he could have at least hung around to meet the team," Lanie mutters, clearly disappointed by Colton's disappearing act.

"I'm sure we'll see him bright and early tomorrow," I reply, pulling off my cap and dipping my head backward into the cool liquid of the pool.

This is my favorite part of practice—the part where I release my hair and let it flow like a damp curtain down my shoulders and back.

Bliss.

It's such a small thing, but it reminds me of summers back at the lake. My lips curl with the fond memories of floating in the water with my mom, tanning our too-pale skin to a rosy pink just to irritate my dad.

"Y'all are gonna get cancer," he always said.

"Nah, sunscreen will do us right," my mom would reply.

I grin and eventually tuck my legs beneath me to stand. Lanie and Jesi have already run off to the showers, leaving me to my little after-practice ritual. It's my thing. My moment of peace. My way of remembering the parents I lost too many years ago.

Miss you, I tell them as I pull myself up onto the deck.

With a sigh, I shut my eyes and roll my neck, loosening it. The silence in the natatorium puts me at ease, just like the soothing texture of the water against my skin as I swim.

It's my home.

My safe place.

My haven.

No one can disturb me here. And yet, a deep tone dares to try as someone says, "Your walls could use some work."

My brow furrows as I open my eyes to find Colton Kinsley leaning against the block by lane one, his jean-clad legs crossed at the ankles and showcasing a fancy pair of black boots.

I consider his words and nod. "I know." Walls are my weakness, especially during a distance practice. I breathe too much and kick too little.

"Then why aren't you trying to fix it?" he asks, the lilt in his words betraying a slight English accent.

I've spent so much time studying his stroke that I've never actually heard him speak before. Interviews bore me, and he tends to avoid them anyway.

"Who says I'm not?" I counter, walking over to the towel rack.

"The performance I just watched," he says, pushing off the block to follow me.

We're the only two left on the deck, everyone else having disappeared into the locker rooms before I slipped out of the pool.

"Your form is decent," he continues. "Your

turns are weak."

I pick up the warm cotton to dab it against my face, then rotate to find him right behind me. "They're not weak. They're just not as solid as they could be."

"They're weak," he insists. "They'll cost you the trial, too. As will this laissez-faire approach to practice. Showing up exhausted before it already starts? What the hell were you thinking?"

Okay, wow. So much for the "nice guy" reputation. "Is this attitude 'cause I disturbed your peace in the pool?" I ask. "Or is this your version of being charmin'?"

"The words you're searching for are *because* and *charming*," he retorts. "And if anyone will be charming anyone, it'll be *you* charming *me*. Now go take a shower. We have somewhere to be."

I blink at him. "Excuse me? We don't even know each other."

"On the contrary, Emma Adrian, I know everything about you. And I have to say, I'm not impressed with what I have to work with."

"Well, I'm not all that impressed right now either," I admit. "You can't just hog the pool. I get that you're a swimming god, but we had a scheduled practice. So I'm not gonna apologize for jumping in when I did."

"*Going to*," he corrects. "And I don't give a damn about your practice, Adrian. In fact, the only thing you did today that impressed me was jumping into the pool when you did. It all went to hell from there. Drifting off your teammates won't help you win the trial. You need to drown them in your wake instead."

"I see." I flash him my best sweet Southern smile. "Well, thank you for the advice, Mister Kinsley. The next time I want guidance from an asshole, I'll be sure to look you up." I give him a little finger wave. "You take care now, ya hear?"

I start by him, only to find my wrist caught in his hand.

"This isn't a joke, Adrian."

"I prefer 'Emma,'" I fire back as I try to dislodge his hold. He walks me back into the wall instead, his body towering over mine.

His minty aftershave makes me a little dizzy as I steal a deep breath, but I do my best not to show my reaction to his clean scent.

"Release me."

"You don't seem to be hearing me, *Emma*. You're my charge. I'm going to guide you. If you fail, it's your life on the line, not mine. I'm an Elder's son. I'm already inducted. You're just a recruit."

"A recruit?" My eyebrows shoot upward. "I'm a team member already. Freshman. Enrolled. And I don't know what you mean by *Elder*, but good for you." I look him over. "As for being in charge of me, I don't think so." I yank my wrist from him, but his grip tightens. "Let. Me. Go."

His eyes narrow as he searches my expression. Whatever he sees there has him cursing out a breath. "You have no idea..."

I arch a brow. "Excuse me?"

He just shakes his head. "I'm going to fucking kill Connor." He pushes away from me to run his fingers through his dark hair. "Go get dressed. We'll talk afterward."

"Sure," I drawl. "We'll do that."

We absolutely will *not* be doing that.

Because I have plans.

And they do not involve meeting up with a jackass named Colton Kinsley.

Cheese on a cracker. I chose Stonewall University because of this guy? The supposed swimming god? Ugh, and he turns out to be the biggest asshat on the planet.

Great.

Just my luck.

I grab another towel on my way off the deck, Colton's tones following behind me as he says, "You fucking dick." I glance over my shoulder, curious to see if he's talking to himself—because those words seem to apply just fine.

But no.

He's on the phone.

"This isn't fucking funny," he continues.

I roll my eyes and leave him to it.

Rather than shower and change in the locker room, I tug on a pair of sweats and a sweatshirt over my suit, put on some sneakers, grab my bag, and head toward the exit. The girls are all gossiping in the showers as I leave, their topic one I definitely don't want to discuss.

What the hell just happened?

I finally met my idol, and he turned out to be a colossal ass. He didn't even introduce himself, just started into me on my technique.

Okay, yeah, I probably could have worked a little harder today. And yeah, I showed up tired. But it's one practice. I'm allowed a bad day.

And it wasn't even that bad. I still came in first at the wall for almost every set.

My heart beats a little harder as I head back to my dorm, my mind spinning.

For months, I looked forward to that moment. I anticipated a lot of exchanges, all of them around technique and training and advice on how to mentally prepare for a race. Not one of them went in this direction, with Colton being a complete and utter dick.

I understand arrogance. I respect pride and skill. But this is something else entirely.

He was... angry? Cruel? Harsh?

All of the above.

I shake my head as I pick up the pace, my legs suddenly restless like I have all this energy to burn despite the exhausting practice I just went through.

At least Rylie will be pleased.

I promised to attend some fight with her tonight. Not our usual Friday evening activity, but she heard about it from someone on campus, and she's obsessed with finding out why people would actively engage in such violence.

And she's recruited me to go with her.

Like a good friend and roommate, I've agreed.

Something I'm oddly happy about now because I could use some violence in my life. Preferably my fist meeting Colton Kinsley's face.

My lips twitch at the thought as I pick up my pace into a jog.

Yeah, some bloody fighting sounds pretty good right about now.

CHAPTER TWO

Emma

"This is insane," I shout to Rylie. There are people everywhere, and the room is crawling with testosterone. Well, *room* isn't accurate. It's more like a giant warehouse with a ring at the center. Two guys are beating the shit out of each other. No surprise there, as it's been that way since we arrived. Just a revolving door of fighters trying to win in the makeshift ring. However, something about these new guys seems to have upped the excitement in the air.

I don't know much about fighting, but I can tell he's popular.

Or maybe hated.

Regardless, he's big and intimidating, and he has an evil smirk as he eyes his opponent.

I shiver.

This is definitely not my scene. And it's not

Rylie's either, but she seems enthralled by the crowd. "You're doing that psych thing again, aren't you?" I ask against her ear. Her parents are both psychologists, and, shocker, she's a psych major, too. And now she's studying the people with a rapt expression, her hazel irises analyzing their every move.

I groan. "I should have known that was why you wanted to do this." She is obsessed with psychoanalyzing everyone and everything.

When I confided in her about the death of my parents—and the fact that it had happened when I was twelve—she wanted to know every detail. And it wasn't the sincere curiosity of an innocent asking about how they had died. No, she inquired about my feelings and my reactions, and then she ascertained that I would do.

Like I passed some sort of test.

I decided at that moment that she wasn't like most girls. And, well, I suppose she passed my test, too, because now we are close friends. Time didn't seem to matter. We just got each other.

"This is fascinating," she tells me. Her chestnut hair is piled into a messy bun on top of her head. The relaxed style pairs well with her attire of muck boots, jeans, and a hoodie. She once mentioned something about being from Maine, like that explained her clothing preferences.

Mine have nothing to do with my home state.

Southern Georgia is all about sunshine, not rain. And we certainly don't need a lot of sweaters. But up here in New York? Yeah, this is a whole new world for me. Hence my sweater, jeans, thick socks, and heeled boots. I almost brought a coat as well, but Rylie thought it would be a little hot in here.

She was right.

It burns like a hot summer day in here with all the people crowding around to watch a bunch of sweaty men fight.

"Certainly not in Savannah anymore," I mutter to myself.

"I heard that," Rylie replies.

"Of course you did. Selective hearing and all." I grin at her, but the people yelling around us draw her attention back to the stage. I flinch as the big dude takes a harsh hit to the jaw, blood spewing from his lips as he falls to the side.

The realistic vision puts my daydream of punching Colton to shame. Mostly because my version lacked blood.

Shouts of triumph go through the crowd, followed by groans and curses.

A shiver trickles up my spine at the mounting aggression in the air. A few of the guys nearby shove at each other for messing up a bet. Or I think that might be the case. Their words are slurred with booze, the alcohol heavy in the atmosphere.

"Uh, Ry?" I say, using my preferred nickname for her. "Maybe we should...?" I trail off as a group of people start chanting at the stage.

Big Guy is back on his feet and looks hella pissed about taking one to the jaw.

I instinctively take a step back, but Rylie is under some sort of trance. Her fascination is written in her elven features, her petite frame thrumming with curiosity.

My stomach churns with discomfort. I'm not a naïve little bluebell, but I'm not all that experienced either. Especially not with this.

Swimmers don't fight. We're competitive to an extent, but we come together for relays and understand the value of working as a team.

These two guys on the stage are not teammates.

They look ready to kill each other, and suddenly I'm afraid we're all about to bear witness to a crime. Big Guy has murder written into his expression, his bald head glistening in the dull lights above.

I take another step back, directly into a hard chest. With my heart in my throat, I jump forward while mouthing an apology, only to be secured with a hand on my hip.

"Well, this isn't where I wanted to have this conversation," a deep voice says against my ear. "But it'll do."

"C-Colton?" I stammer, glancing over my

shoulder.

"It's rude not to watch," he tells me as his opposite hand goes to my chin to force my eyes back to the stage. "Who do you want to win?"

"I…" I swallow. "What are you doing here?"

"Looking for you," he says.

"Wh-what? Why?" It comes out hoarse, his nearness paired with our surroundings leaving me off-kilter. *He's here for me?*

The palm on my hip shifts to my abdomen to hold me more firmly against the muscular god behind me while his other hand remains on my chin, forcing me to watch the fight.

"We have a lot to discuss, little pledge." His lips graze my ear. "Starting with ground rules. So I suggest you enjoy what you're about to witness, as it'll be the last fight you'll be allowed to see for the next five months."

"Excuse me?" I try to move, but his arm locks around my abdomen, his strength bleeding into me through the thick layers of our clothes. "Colton—"

"Watch," he demands.

I want to argue, but the cheering grows as Big Guy slams his fist into his opponent with a victorious roar.

Except he celebrates too soon, because in the next second, the smaller fighter sends an uppercut to Big Guy's chin, followed by a chop to his throat.

Silence falls as everyone holds their breath.

And the smaller opponent adds a final blow to Big Guy's head.

It all happens in a few blinks but plays out in slow motion.

Then Big Guy tips over and down he goes, his hefty form crashing into the floor with a resounding thud.

Colton snorts as the crowd goes wild.

I search for Rylie, my heart in my throat. Everyone is losing their damn minds, stirring an unruly atmosphere that screams danger to my senses.

"Rylie!" I yell.

But she's lost to the crowd, observing as the chaos unfolds.

"Let go," I tell Colton, desperate to reach Rylie.

"No."

"No?" Is he joking right now? I look sharply over my shoulder, managing to release my chin from his grip. "Do you manhandle all women, or am I just an unlucky victim?"

His dark eyes smolder. "If I don't manhandle you, someone else will."

"Excuse me?" Pretty sure that's the second time I've used that phrase with him today.

"You're an innocent little Southern belle in the middle of an illegal fight club," he says. "You're fight bait."

"Fight bait?" I repeat with a humorless laugh. "I don't—"

A shriek pierces the air nearby, sending a chill down my spine. My attention shifts sideways just in time to see Rylie go barreling through a crowd of men and women. She walks right up to Big Guy—who is no longer on the stage—and kicks him square in the balls.

I gasp as he falls to his knees.

And my eyes widen as she slams the heel of her muck boot against his throat.

"Oh, hell," I breathe, now even more desperate to get to her. But Colton refuses to budge. "Let go of me!" I demand.

A few people cast curious looks our way but say nothing. Like it's entirely normal to be held against my will.

What is wrong with these people?

No, better question: *What is wrong with Colton Kinsley?*

Sure, he's a swimming god and the son of one of the most powerful attorneys in the world. But this is next-level arrogance.

I'm about to tell him off as a dark-haired male with ice-blue eyes joins the scene with Rylie. His irises flash as he glances my way, then his focus shifts to the male behind me. Something seems to pass through the air, because the dark-haired one gives a subtle nod.

"Your friend will be fine," Colton says against

my ear. "Well, unless the Scorpio Society taps her, too. Then I can't guarantee anything."

"The what?"

"Come on, little pledge." He starts walking me backward with both his arms locked around my waist. "Time for that chat."

I dig in my heels, refusing to move. "I'm not going anywhere with you. And I'm definitely not leaving Rylie with that guy." He's over six feet of solid muscle, and he's looking at my friend with a calculating gleam that leaves me uneasy.

Then Colton shifts me back another step, and I lose sight of her.

"She'll be okay," he says against my ear. "Trust me."

"Trust you?" I laugh. "Right. I don't know you, Colton. And what little I did know about you is clearly incorrect. You can swim; I'll give you that. But you're not a nice guy. Nor do you seem to be all that shy." A fact I've learned with all his manhandling.

If I don't manhandle you, someone else will.

What kind of lame excuse is that, anyway?

He called me *fight bait*. An innocent Southern belle.

I'll show him *innocent*.

He begins to speak, but I'm done listening to him.

I stomp back on his toe with my heel and introduce my elbow to his ribs. His responding growl has me repeating both actions as I try to fight my way out of his hold.

A few people start to watch. Not help. Just *watch*. Like they're amused by my show of strength. That only pisses me off more.

At least until I notice some of the hungry gleams coming from the men in the crowd. Their eyes are roaming over me with clear interest, their tongues snaking out to dampen their bottom lips.

Uh…

A few others elbow each other with chuckles, their gazes tracking over my movements before evaluating the male behind me.

I stop struggling.

These guys are big. Not as tall as Colton, but definitely bulkier. His arms clamp around me like cement, and I allow it because I prefer his manhandling over their intrigue.

Except they don't seem to care that he's the one holding me. Two of them step forward, cruel smiles on their lips. "Well, what do we have here? A fresh dove?"

"Fuck off, Jimmy," Colton says.

The bulky bald guy only grins more. "Your girl doesn't seem to want me to fuck off, Kinsley. I think she wants *you* to fuck off."

"She's off-limits," another voice says, his tone deep and underlined with authority. "And you should know better than to challenge a Kinsley, especially in *my* club."

"Not yours yet, Hawthorne," one of the men mutters.

"You want to say that to my face?" The icy-blue-eyed guy from earlier steps up beside us. "No? I didn't think so." He looks directly at Colton. "Get her out of here."

"Trying to," Colton says. "But she's freaking out over her friend."

"Her friend is fine." Icy Eyes, who I'm guessing goes by *Hawthorne*, pulls Rylie into view with his hand clamped down around her upper arm.

"Ry," I breathe, trying futilely to reach for her.

Her hazel irises hold a hardness to them, her irritation evident. Not with me, but with whatever the hell just happened back there. "I'm okay, Em."

"We need to go," I say.

"No." Hawthorne's tone leaves no room for argument. "*Ry* and I are going to have a word."

Rylie glances up at him, her expression filled with a notoriously wondrous look. Even caught in the death grip of what appears to be a devilish creature, she's still enthralled by mental motivations.

"Ry—"

"I'll meet you back at the dorm," she interjects, her resolve palpable.

I groan. There's no talking sense into her when she's in this sort of mood. She's on a mission—one I'll never understand—and trying to fight her on it will just end in her doing it anyway.

"Good choice," Icy Eyes says darkly. He glances at the guys who haven't backed off yet and arches a single dark brow. "Didn't I tell you to fuck off?"

Colton grunts. "No, but I did."

"And they should fucking listen." Icy Eyes stares the others down until they take a few steps back.

And Rylie observes with severe interest.

Great.

"Those wolves would eat you alive," Colton says against my ear. "Now let's go."

Icy Eyes steers Rylie away from me while Colton speaks, leaving me without much of an option. Either stay and face the *wolves,* as he called them, or obey his command.

My jaw ticks.

I don't like demands.

But I also don't want to be "eaten alive."

So I opt to let him guide me outside instead. Mostly because I'm hoping he'll let me go the second we step into the night. But he doesn't. He guides me to an expensive-looking coupe instead. "Get in," he tells me.

"I'd rather walk."

"You need to save your legs for practice in the morning," he replies, opening the door to his sporty black car. "And I wasn't asking; I was telling."

I spin around to face him. "I'm all for a gentleman who opens doors, but I don't do the commanding alpha thing." Well, not that I know of, anyway. I've not dated much. Swimming is my first and only love. I refuse to accept distractions, and boyfriends certainly qualify as one.

He clenches his teeth, his cheekbones seeming to become more pronounced in the process. Colton really is a handsome man, with those dark brows, stubbled jawline, and perfect facial structure. However, behind the sexy mask is an alpha asshole who manhandles women and issues demands instead of requests.

If I had a type, it wouldn't be this.

I fold my arms and stare up at him.

He stares back, his dark eyes narrowing.

After a beat, he sighs and shakes his head. "Please get in the car."

My eyebrows wing upward. "So you do know kind words? Fascinating. But the answer is still no."

He releases a low growl, his palm coming up to rest on the top of his car while his other hand remains on the door, effectively caging me in against the coupe. "All right. This hasn't started the way it should have, and for that, I'm sorry.

But I really need you to get in the car, Emma. We need to talk."

"About what?"

"Something I can't comment on out here," he says, glancing around the parking lot. There are several people lingering around. No one appears to be actively listening to us, but that doesn't mean they can't hear us. "Please, Emma. I know I haven't given you the best first impression, but I'm not a complete ass. I thought you knew... and I've since realized you don't." He removes his hand from the car to pinch the bridge of his nose, his expression taking on one of regret mingled with exhaustion. "Just... get in the car. Please."

All right, that's two instances of a *please* and an apology.

His facial features also appear adequately contrite.

If it were anyone else, I'd walk.

But Colton Kinsley isn't anyone else. And while he's been a total ass, it's not like he's a complete stranger.

I'm also a bit intrigued by what he has to say. "Where are you gonna take me?"

"My place," he says.

I blanch.

He rolls his eyes. "Not for sex, but to eat and talk."

Okay, sex isn't what I thought at all. It was

just instinctual to react to Colton Kinsley saying he's taking me back to his place.

However, now I'm thinking about the alternatives to that phrase—thanks to his comment—and I'm not sure how I feel about them.

"Emma," he prompts. "*Please*."

"Three times?" I'm almost impressed. "Well, you know what they say about it being the *charm* and all that." I shrug and slide into the leather bucket seat.

He says something under his breath that I don't catch and shuts the door behind me.

I'm totally going to regret this.

However, seeing one of his medals may make it worth it.

I make a mental note to ask. Then I buckle myself in for the ride.

CHAPTER THREE

Colton

My grip tightens around the steering wheel as I drive.

I don't have time for this. Any of it. Emma. Family obligations. Scorpio Society bullshit. Fuck, all I want to do is jump into the water and make some waves. But no, I'm stuck here in this damn M4 with a gorgeous little Southern belle beside me.

At least she's nice to look at.

Her skill in the pool isn't bad either. Except for her turns—those need serious work.

And I have five months to fix them.

Shit.

She says nothing as I drive, giving me time to formulate my explanation. Connor was supposed to do this part, but the prick left the job to me. Considering the desired outcome of this situation, I expected him to at least help.

However, no. He's too busy with his caseload to try.

And, as he so kindly pointed out, it's my turn to take on the family mantle. He let me *play* for long enough—his term, not mine. Because the Olympics are a game, not a true achievement.

Dick, I think, wanting to punch him all over again.

I've avoided the Scorpio Society obligations since my freshman year of college. After passing my induction—with my brother serving as my Capo—the society gave me leave to pursue my Olympic career. My father has a whole fleet of Soldiers to help with inductions. He also has my brother.

But then my mother chose Emma as a pledge.

And my father and brother called me back to help serve as her Capo.

She's a swimmer. A good one. An Olympic hopeful. The perfect asset for the Kinsley family. Not even an asset, but a trophy.

Because we need more of those.

I almost roll my eyes, but I'm too focused on the road to try.

Emma shifts beside me, her floral scent taunting my nose. She really is a little Southern flower, all soft petals and tender perfection. I can see why my mother chose her. She's an ideal match.

And not mine.

Which is fine.

But I'm the one charged with ensuring she survives.

"I thought you knew," I say, feeling the need to apologize again. It's a foreign sensation. I don't usually screw something up this badly upon a first—and second—meeting.

I'm not a complete nitwit. I know how to talk to women. However, this whole situation is suffocating me. I don't want to be here. I don't want to do this to her. Yet I have no choice. And she doesn't either.

"Thought I knew what?" she asks, her voice softer now that we're alone. More intimate. Her Southern drawl is growing on me every time she speaks, too. It's endearing, giving her a sweetness that I don't want to like. Which is why I lashed out earlier by correcting her.

I don't want to like this girl.

She's my charge. My task. Nothing more.

And if she doesn't do what I tell her to, she'll die.

"Thought I knew what?" she repeats, drawing me back to her.

I clear my throat. "About the Scorpio Society."

Her confused silence tells me she knows nothing about it. But I already knew that after witnessing her reaction to my words earlier.

"My brother was supposed to tell you," I continue. "But apparently he didn't. And the asshole failed to mention that to me." It's just like Connor, too. He loves fucking with me. I suppose that's a prerequisite for being an older sibling. "So when I saw you at the pool, I thought you were aware of why I was back. Which is why I didn't bother with an introduction and jumped right in on my critique."

We don't have a lot of time for her to achieve perfection, so the faster she learns, the better. But that all requires her to be a willing pupil.

"You've been chosen, Emma," I tell her as I turn onto my street. It's just off campus, making it an easy five-minute drive to the natatorium. And like Stonewall University, it's an affluent area. Actually, everything near the grounds is rich and beautiful because the Scorpio Society owns all the land.

We own Stonewall, too. The dean is an Elder. It makes admissions and recruitment easier. The society handpicks all the potential recruits, ensures they enroll, and then selects the most eligible freshmen to pledge.

Those who pass the tests are inducted.

Those who don't... die.

And it's the job of the Soldiers to test the potential members. Unless a situation like mine arises, and it goes to a Capo, otherwise known as a General.

I'm technically not a Capo.

But I am the son of an Elder.

Which gives me certain perks and leeway among the society because I'm a legacy—the son of one of the twelve original families.

A Kinsley heir.

My older brother may be the next in line, but I'm the spare. If anything happens to him, or should he choose to step down, I'm up on deck.

Yay me.

I pull into my driveway, the garage automatically opening to accept my entry. Emma remains utterly still beside me, her tension thickening the air in the car. "I'm not going to hurt you," I promise. "But I am going to push you." Because that's my job.

The door begins to close behind us as I turn off the car.

She's barely breathing—not a great sign since I haven't even begun to explain the Scorpio Society.

"Let's go inside," I suggest, unbuckling my seat belt.

She doesn't move.

Yeah, this is off to a fabulous start. "I don't know how to do this," I admit, rubbing my hand over my face before gripping the back of my neck. "I knew about the Scorpio Society at birth. My father's an Elder, one of the original twelve families, and so I always knew my fate. And not passing the tests seemed like an impossibility. Although, my test was similar to yours—a show of dedication."

Exactly four years ago.

My first Olympic year.

And now she's destined to follow in my footsteps.

"It's why they want me to mentor you. Or rather, to be your Capo. To test you. It's my job to push you to be the best. If you fail, well…" I trail off, not really wanting to focus on that. "My point is, I'm here to be a guide. But I'm also your warden."

My palm falls from my nape as I blow out a long breath.

She's still not moving.

And I'm really not explaining this well.

"You're familiar with Greek life, right? Like, rushing a sorority?" I glance at her. She doesn't say anything, but her brow furrows, so I know she's listening. "Think of this like that, except it's a secret society that no one knows about. Only those worthy of pledging are tapped, and you've been hand-selected by the Kinsley family to rush. Which means you have to go through the ritual and trials to be formally inducted."

She swallows, her gaze finally sliding over to meet mine. Dubiousness radiates from her dark depths, and I know she's questioning my sanity. I don't blame her. It's a lot to take in as an outsider.

"The Scorpio Society selects rushees from all backgrounds," I explain. "They like diversity. But the primary goal is to establish connections with the elite of the world, or those in power positions. Or those who might achieve greatness, like an Olympic hopeful."

I capture and hold her gaze, needing her to hear me and to understand.

"They select the best of the best, Emma. Then they test those recruits, and those who pass are inducted into one of the world's most elite societies. You'll have access to anything and everything you could possibly dream of. It's an extremely connected, affluential world. And you've been tapped to join it."

Her expression tells me she doesn't believe a word I'm saying to her.

If my brother had done his job, this wouldn't be an issue.

"All right." I pick up my phone and scroll through my contact list. "You're familiar with Dean Stonewall, right?"

She snorts in response.

"That's what I thought." I dial his direct line and wait a beat for him to answer.

"Kinsley," he says as his face appears on my screen. "It's late."

"I know," I reply. "This will only take a

second." I tilt the phone so Emma can see my screen. Her eyebrows shoot upward as she recognizes the man on my screen.

When Dean Stonewall's green eyes find hers, his own salt-and-pepper eyebrows arch upward. "Emma Adrian."

Her lips part in surprise. "D-Dean," she stammers out.

At least she's found her voice, I think.

Then I focus on Jonathan Stonewall and explain the reason for my call. "Connor failed to inform her of her fate. I've told her she's been tapped by the Scorpio Society, and she thinks I've lost my mind."

He considers me for a moment before glancing toward her again. "Well, welcome to the Scorpio Society, Emma. I suggest you listen to your Capo and do exactly what he says." He looks at me. "Anything else?"

I study her shocked expression as I reply, "No, I think that'll do for now. Thank you, sir."

"Kinsley."

"Dean Stonewall."

The line clicks as he ends the call.

And Emma just gapes at my phone like it's some sort of magical wand.

"The Stonewalls are one of the founding families, just like mine. Roman—the man who took an interest in your roommate tonight—is from another. He's a Hawthorne. There are nine others. I'm sure you'll meet them with time, assuming you pass your trials. Which I'll tell you more about in my kitchen." I skipped dinner tonight while tracking her down, and I really need to eat something.

That's the thing with swimmers—we're always hungry.

I don't wait for her to comply this time. I merely open my door, exit, and head into my house. The alarm is already off, thanks to the proximity of my phone.

I set my wallet and keys on the table in my mud room, then enter my dining area. It opens into my kitchen and the living room, providing a spacious and welcoming interior.

A master bedroom is across the floor plan, with three more rooms upstairs, and a basement underneath. I may show her that later, as I suspect she'll like it down there because I have a custom-built lap pool meant for training.

As I told her in the car, the Scorpio Society is affluent. As is my family.

She doesn't come inside right away, giving me time to pull an already prepared dinner from the fridge. Zarah left it for me earlier, the contents suitable for two because I anticipated Emma joining me after practice.

Then the little vixen ran off to her dorm.

And disappeared with her roommate.

Roman texted shortly after, asking if I

lost something, then sent through a photo of my charge. He knew my family tapped her for initiation, and also knew I would not approve of her attending a fight night in the middle of swim season.

So I left dinner behind to go searching for the pretty little brunette.

Which caused me to starve in the process.

Brat, I think, sliding the pasta dish into the oven to reheat it. As Emma likely didn't have a proper meal earlier either, I grab her a plate and silverware and set them on the table inside my kitchen nook. It's a little more peaceful and framed by a window overlooking the trees, as opposed to my dining area with floor-to-ceiling glass doors that open to my deck out back.

My mother bought me a ten-person table for that space—a complete waste of money, as I don't often allow others into the sanctuary of my home.

Emma will become an exception because we have a lot of work to do and very little time to do it.

The female in question finally decides to come inside as I'm setting two glasses of ice water on the table. Her brow furrows at the sight, then her nose crinkles as the aroma of tomatoes and garlic begins to flood my kitchen space.

"I assume you're hungry?" I phrase it as a question even though it's more of a statement.

She doesn't reply, just steps into my kitchen with a bemused expression on her face.

"Did you try calling for help?" I wonder out loud, aware that she has a phone in her pocket.

Her expression tells me she didn't even consider it. A good thing because there's no one who can help her now.

"I can see that you didn't, which is good," I say, returning to check on the dinner in the oven. "The Scorpio Society has contacts in a lot of high places." The food isn't quite ready, so I lean my hip against the counter beside it and meet her dark brown eyes. "I don't recommend going to the police. They can't help you. And the society will punish you for it, likely with your life."

She blinks.

I stare.

Then I sigh and run my fingers through my hair. It's soft, thanks to the expensive products I use to kill the chlorine.

After a beat of silence, I push off the counter to stand in front of her. "Look, I know this all sounds unbelievable or maybe even scary, but the Scorpio Society is an organization of prestige and substantial wealth. You'll have access to whatever you want. You just have to pass the trials."

I can see by her expression that I'm not selling her on anything.

"Whatever I want," she repeats. "At the

expense of what?"

An intelligent and fair question, one that deserves an honest response.

"At the expense of potentially losing your life," I answer. "The trials will either make... or break you."

In her case, I hope for the former but fear for the latter.

This won't be easy.

I need her trust to be able to guide her.

And something tells me that's going to be our biggest challenge in this situation. Particularly as she's glowering at me now when she should be showing some respect.

I'm not just an Olympian; I'm Clive Kinsley's son. We're a founding family, and my father serves as one of the twelve Elders of the society.

That alone makes most members bow in my presence.

But Emma isn't fazed.

She's pissed.

This is going to be a long night.

CHAPTER FOUR

Emma

"So let me make sure I have this straight," I say slowly. "Your family has selected me to join a secret organization, one with *connections* and *wealth*, where I have to pass a series of trials to be formally inducted. And I have no choice or say in the matter. It's already done and expected that I'll just… comply."

"Essentially, yeah." He bends to pull a pan of penne noodles tousled in tomato sauce from the oven.

My nose crinkles at his choice in reheating a pasta dish in such a manner. A skillet would have been a better option. However, the scents filling the air are appetizing enough. Given that he set two plates, I assume he wants me to eat with him. On principle, I should decline. But my stomach prefers that I accept. As do my manners.

My grandma raised me to always appreciate and accept hospitality, even when I want to decline.

I'm doing this for you, I think at her. She's my only living relative and the reason I've been able to train. She took me in after my parents died. She raised me and then sent me off to Stonewall.

To be recruited against my will into a secret society with affluent connections.

How… fortuitous.

He asked if I tried calling for help. Who would I call? The police? And say what?

Five-time Olympic gold medalist Colton Kinsley says I've been tapped to join a super-secret club that, oh, by the way, the dean knows about. He says it's a matter of life or death, and I have to pass some sort of test where he's making me… I frown. *Making me what?*

"What's my test?" I ask out loud as he sets the pans on a mitt in the center of the table.

"Sit and I'll tell you."

My jaw clenches. "Don't command me like some sort of pet."

"I wouldn't dream of it. Dogs are far better behaved," he drawls, taking over the head of the table. Then he gestures to the other place setting with an expectant look.

Part of me wants to pick up the pasta dish and dump it over his arrogant head.

The other part of me wants to eat and find out more about this test so I can potentially talk my way out of it.

What does he want me to do? What could I possibly have to give an organization like the one he described?

My grandpa owned a construction company down south that made decent money, but it wasn't Kinsley-level money. Just enough to live comfortably.

Colton serves himself a reasonable helping of pasta, then he stands again.

I move on instinct, half expecting him to grab me.

He gives me a chiding look before going to the fridge to pull out two bowls of already prepared salads. "What kind of dressing do you want?" he asks after setting them on the table. "I have a sweet vinaigrette, olive oil with spices, and regular Italian. Oh, and Greek, too." He opens the door to his fridge again to show me.

"Greek," I whisper, my heart skipping a beat. "You expected me to come over for dinner." It's not a question because his food preparation already tells me he anticipated company tonight. And he asked me to join him after practice.

"Yes." He grabs the Greek dressing and shuts the fridge. "As I said earlier, I thought you already knew about your recruitment. My brother was supposed to handle that part. I'm here to coach and help."

"Coach and help me to do what exactly?" I follow him to the table this time and sit before he can tell me to.

His lips quirk up into a partial grin as he sets the dressing on the table. Then he steals my plate to put a healthy portion on it. "I know you're allergic to shellfish, so this is all beef-based," he says as he sets the dish in front of me. "Same with the salad and dressing, obviously."

He returns to his chair as I gape at him. "You know I'm allergic to shellfish?"

"As I also mentioned earlier, I know everything about you, Emma Adrian." He takes a napkin from the table and places it in his lap. "I spent the holidays studying your records to ensure everything I do and advise helps you more than hurts you. And had I known you weren't aware of your future, I would have approached today very differently."

He grimaces with that statement.

Then he picks up his water and downs half of it.

"As to your test, it's fairly straightforward," he continues. "You need to qualify for the Olympics in five individual events. Do that, and you're in. Don't, and the Olympics will be the least of your concerns."

"*Five* individual events?" I repeat, gaping at him. That will require me to place in the top two spots in all my events. "I've qualified for the trials in seven. I-I'm only seated in the top two for three of them right now."

And that's being generous, considering Molly Black is only a hundredth behind me in the hundred butterfly.

"That's why I'm here." His voice is soft and at odds with his hard expression. "It won't be easy, but it wouldn't be a test if it was." He says this like it's perfectly normal and acceptable to expect me to just acquiesce to the terms.

Five Olympic qualifications.

Sure.

No problem.

I want to strangle him. Instead, I ask an intelligent counterquestion: "Why five individuals? Why not three individual events and two relays?"

He snorts. "That's not a true challenge. You're already noted as a likely candidate for the two hundred fly and four hundred individual medley. To round it out, you need three more. The Scorpio Society expects *the best,* Emma. Therefore, it's five individual events. No negotiations allowed."

"I suppose you'll tell me which events next?" I voice the query with a sarcastic lilt that makes him grin.

"No. I'll let you choose. Although, I don't recommend breaststroke. Your legs don't appreciate that stroke." He spears his salad and brings a bite to his mouth.

I've suddenly lost my appetite.

Five events. It's something I've fantasized about for the future. As in four and a half years from now. It's part of my plan—get my feet wet at the Olympics after my freshman year, then train hard for the next four years with swimmers like Colton, and achieve the dream at the next Olympics.

In four and a half years, I repeat to myself. *Not this year.*

My head is spinning.

It's an impossible task.

He has to know that.

"It's not negotiable," he says again, probably because he can see the doubt in my features.

"Colton—"

"We already broke one rule for your initiation by extending the timetable for your induction. Most initiates attend a ceremony at the end of the semester. But the trials are in June. So you'll be inducted afterward, assuming you qualify."

"This is insane."

He shrugs. "Life is insane. But it's also worth noting that I passed a similar test four years ago. Be thankful they're not requiring five golds from you."

I gape at him. "You... five...?" I can't even voice it. But I understand the implication. "The Olympics was your test." The words leave my mouth on a breath, my voice barely audible.

"Tests provide motivation," he replies,

meeting my gaze. "I don't regret it. And to be honest, I miss the pressure. Swimming isn't just about skill. It takes mental strength, too."

I don't speak, but I silently agree. It's easy to psych out before a race. Knowing a life may be on the line could provide a heck of a lot of motivation.

Or destroy a mindset.

"Eat," he says softly. "That's not a command but a request. The sauce has a lot of vitamins in it from crushed vegetables, and the meat is prime, too. It'll help give you energy for practice in the morning, which we both know will be a killer because Coach Hawkins loves Saturday morning death sets."

I flinch. I've experienced a few of those infamous "death sets" this season. My body is not a fan.

Colton grins at my reaction, then he finishes off his salad.

Watching him eat serves no logical purpose whatsoever, so I join him and begrudgingly admit that the food is good.

He definitely didn't make this. It's not that I doubt his skill, but a man like Colton doesn't have time to prepare something this intricate and delicious. It looks easy, but he's right about the vegetables. They're all cooked into the sauce... because it's homemade from scratch.

"Zarah." He utters the name before scooping

up penne into his mouth.

I frown. "What?"

He chews and swallows. "She's my nutritionist and personal chef. She preps all my meals. She's going to start prepping yours, too. That campus crap isn't good enough. Not for your purposes, anyway. She's already working on this week's meal plan."

He wrongly interprets my resounding silence as acceptance and continues into "our" plans.

I'll start training with him tomorrow. He's already spoken to Coach Hawkins, phrasing it as an opportunity to foster upcoming Olympic talent.

"Naturally, he agreed," Colton adds before diving into my revised practice schedule.

Which includes dropping one of my classes.

"Having to run halfway across campus to make it to the natatorium on time is dangerous—winter in upstate New York can be brutal at times—and pushing your limits outside of the pool is unnecessarily exhausting, unless it's cross-training related."

I'm struggling not to throw my plate at him.

And he's not done.

He starts talking about "the rules." No more late-night fight club visits. Absolutely no parties. No alcohol or drugs. No fraternization with men unless I'm properly protected—an act that is none of his damn business. And lastly, I have a curfew of ten o'clock every evening. Nine o'clock on meet nights.

I've only finished half my food, something he notes, so he adds a lecture on the importance of healthy eating when training at the Olympic level.

He speaks like I don't know how to take proper care of myself.

It's insulting.

I know how to cook healthy meals. I know what to eat. I'm well versed in training. And I know about protection!

My fingers are curled into tight fists in my lap, my instinct to punch him riding my spirit hard.

He takes a sip of his water and calmly sets it down. "All right, Emma." He meets my gaze. "Go ahead and yell. I can take it."

"Are you sure?" I ask, my voice so sugary sweet that a peach tree may sprout right here in his damn dining room. "Maybe you need to instruct me on how to yell, too? I'm clearly not capable of much in your eyes, what with all the rules and all."

He sighs, and the sound does nothing to cool my ire. "I'm here to help you, which I've said several times now. These rules are for your own benefit. I just want you to win. And I'm not talking about the society test. I'm talking about the trials. You have a lot of talent, Emma. I've seen you compete. You're almost there. I want to push you those few steps more and watch you fly."

Okay, well that certainly does dampen my anger a little. Primarily because I can see the sincerity in his gaze.

"I know you think I'm an ass. I won't say I'm not. But I'm an ass who can help you. And when you think about it, you'll realize this dream is what you already want anyway. The Scorpio Society is just a bonus."

"A bonus that you say will kill me if I don't make the team in five individual events," I mutter.

"You'll appreciate the additional motivation when you're standing on the deck at the Olympics, waiting to swim your first of five events."

"Seven," I counter, lifting my chin. "Relays." I'm just correcting him because I can, not because I think it's possible. But it is part of my lifelong dream.

His dimples flash. "That's the kind of confidence I want to see daily."

I shake my head. "This is—"

"Insane," he finishes for me. "Yes, you mentioned that." He pushes his plate forward to clasp his hands on the table. "It's getting late. How about you sleep on it and we will discuss more after practice." It doesn't sound like a question because it isn't one.

"Fine," I agree, eager to have some space away from him. "Shall I call for a ride, or are you taking me back to my dorm?"

"Neither." He pushes away from the table and stares me down. "You're sleeping in the guest room."

"Like hell I am."

"You prefer my bed?" His eyebrows shoot upward. "I mean, all right. But I sleep naked. And I'll probably end up using you as a body pillow in the middle of the night." His gaze heats as it dances over me. "Make that *definitely*."

I'm so stunned by the forward comment that I'm rendered speechless.

Did Colton Kinsley just proposition me?

He smirks. "It's a joke, pledge. You're sleeping in the guest room."

His words help me find my voice again. "I'm going back to my dorm."

"You're not," he insists. "You're staying here, and I'm driving you to practice tomorrow. You have everything you need in your locker. No dorm required."

"Okay." I stand and walk right up to him, done with this intimidation game. "Maybe you didn't hear me properly because it wasn't up for debate. I'm not staying here."

He wraps his palm around the back of my neck and pulls me flush against him. I glare up at him, refusing to bend. But my heart is beating a mile a minute in my chest because I can feel every inch of his muscular form against mine.

Just like I can smell his minty aftershave.

Fresh and clean, I think, the scent reminding me of a welcoming shower and crisp sheets after a long, grueling practice.

"I don't trust you to go back to your dorm tonight, Emma. Not after everything I've revealed. So you're staying here. We'll discuss next steps after practice."

He releases me as quickly as he grabbed me.

"I've already set an alarm and locked all the doors from my phone. You can't leave even if you tried. Now either follow me or sleep in the living room. Trust me, the guest room is more comfortable, and it's private."

CHAPTER FIVE

Emma

I chose the guest room because it has a door with a lock.

A lock Colton proved to have a key for when he woke me up this morning with a plate of egg whites and a protein shake.

I usually go without breakfast before practice, but I begrudgingly have to admit his meal this morning adequately prepared me for Coach's death sets.

Of course, I'm still sore as hell at the end and just want to be left to die in the pool. I assume my floating position—the one I take after every practice—and close my eyes as everyone disappears into the locker rooms.

Peace.
Tranquility.
Per—

The water ripples around me as someone jumps into the lane beside me.

I groan, irritated by the disturbance.

Then I yelp as that disturbance grabs my ankle and yanks me under the water.

I kick and sputter as I break the surface again, then glare at Colton. His lips curl in response. "Put these back on," he says, handing me my cap and goggles. "We're going to work on flip turns."

I growl at him in response. "Not today."

"Yes, today."

"I'm exhausted."

"Which means your walls will be extraordinarily sloppy." He folds his arms over his chiseled chest. "That's the best time to correct them."

"It's the worst time to correct them because my focus is shot."

"Then re-harness your focus," he returns, impatience thickening his accent. I wonder if he even notices the English inflection in his words. From what little I know about his family, his father is American, so the accent came from either a nanny growing up or his mother.

"Emma," he snaps, looking pointedly at the cap and goggles in my hand. "My time is valuable, and right now you're wasting it."

My eyes narrow. "I didn't ask for your help. Nor do I want it."

His jawbone flexes as he grits his teeth. "Are

the articles wrong about you?"

I blink. "What?"

"The articles—the ones that declare you as an Olympic hopeful—*are they wrong*?"

Now it's my turn to clench my teeth. "Of course they're not wrong."

"Then you want to go to the Olympics?"

"That's why I'm here," I say, waving my free hand at the pool.

"Then why the fuck are we wasting time bickering when you could be swimming?" he demands.

"Because this isn't the way I want to do it," I snap at him.

"Then what way do you prefer?" His tone holds a sardonic twist to it, one that suggests he thinks I'm being petulant. And yeah, maybe I am. But I didn't sign up for this; his family pulled me into it. *Forgive me for not being over that yet.*

"I came here to learn and to train. Not to join a secret society." I lower my voice on that last sentence. The natatorium walls have a way of echoing sometimes, and I don't want those words overheard.

"I fail to see the difference," he says. "You want to go to the Olympics. You want to train. The society just granted you exclusive access to someone who can help guide you there—*me*. So rather than disrespect fate, perhaps you should try accepting it."

"Against my will," I toss back at him. "This is all against my will."

"To help you achieve your true desire!" He blows out a breath and runs a hand over his face, his patience disappearing down the drain of the pool. "I'm here to push you. Most people would see that as the gift that it is. Yes, there are high stakes involved. And yes, that adds pressure. But I've studied you, Emma Adrian, and you thrive best under pressure. So take this experience for what it is, and work with me to achieve greatness."

"At the expense of my coursework and for a prize I don't even want." I shouldn't be arguing with him, because his points are all valid. But I can't get over the notion that this is being forced upon me rather than asked of me.

"Once you're in the Scorpio Society as an inducted member, your coursework won't even matter. You have no idea what kind of resources will become available to you. Just... trust me to guide you, and achieve a dream few others even know exists." There's a subtle plea underlining his tone, one that tells me he genuinely wants me to accept this.

"What's in it for you?" I ask slowly. "You keep saying how this all benefits me, but what about you?"

"I'm doing the work I was called to do," he replies, his voice gruff. "You're not the only one being forced into a situation you may not want, but I learned long ago to accept this life and do what's requested of me when asked."

"So you don't even want to be here either," I translate.

"There are a lot of things I don't want. But I can think of a lot of tasks that are worse than being in the water and sharing the love of my sport with someone who understands my drive and enthusiasm."

A fair argument.

Because I can think of a lot of worse tasks, too.

"What will be required of me when I join?" I ask him.

He considers me for a long moment before replying, "That's not for me to say. All I can tell you is your life will be forever changed, and no one who joins the Scorpio Society is ever sorry for it."

My eyes narrow. "That's a canned response." Which tells me he's hiding something.

He merely lifts a shoulder. "I don't have a better one for you. I'm here to help you pass your trials. This is all about trust, dedication, and perseverance. The rest isn't about us or your tests."

"Trust, dedication, and perseverance," I repeat, arching a brow. "Sounds very specific."

"Those are the pillars chosen for your test, the first one being to trust me to guide you." He gives me a look as he says it, then adds, "It's not going very well so far."

"I wonder why that is?" I counter.

"Because you're being stubborn?" he suggests. "You're choosing to focus on the wrong parts of this equation?" He cocks his head to the side. "Do you realize how many swimmers—hell, how many people in general—would kill for this opportunity? Instead, you've just wasted almost ten minutes of my time by arguing with me about it."

"Comments like that don't make me want to work with you."

He snorts. "Conversations like this don't make me want to coach you, either."

I glare at him.

He just stares right back, unfazed.

The soothing swish of water is the only sound around us, the filters of the pool working to cleanse and replenish in a rhythmic beat.

It's a sound I love, one I've always craved. Because it makes me feel like I'm home and where I belong.

Colton Kinsley has infiltrated that home and disturbed me in his wake. All because of a society I've never heard of, one that apparently wants me to join.

What a heavy burden for him to bear—this secret that he's lived with all his life. Every interview, every meet, every race, this weighs on

COLTON'S SECRET

him.

Five Olympic gold medals achieved for said society. Not for himself, but to prove his worth. "What were your pillars?" I wonder out loud.

He doesn't hesitate. "Loyalty, dedication, and perseverance."

"Loyalty to who?"

"My family legacy," he replies. "To live up to the Kinsley name and achieve greatness."

"Does it bother you?" I ask, my tone a little less hostile and more curious now. Seeing the glimmer in his dark gaze has me clarifying, "Does it bother you that you won five gold medals to satisfy an organization you were essentially born into?"

"Not 'essentially,' I *was* born into it. And no, it doesn't. Because I didn't win those medals for the Scorpio Society. I won them for myself. The rest is just a bonus."

He unfolds his arms to move his palms through the water. At over six feet in height, he can easily stand in this part of the pool. It's only five and a half feet deep here. The deep end would require him to scull like that, but not here. Still, he moves his hands like one would when treading water.

"I'm trying to be patient, Emma," he continues softly. "It doesn't come naturally to me. I'm focused. My drive is what keeps me moving, and I'm not used to being questioned repetitively. I get that this is all new to you, but at the end of the day, it's all meant to encourage you to reach your goals. You enrolled at Stonewall for a reason. You accepted the scholarship for a reason. You're listed as an Olympic hopeful in all the national and international swimming articles *for a reason.*"

I swallow, his words resonating deep within my soul.

The reason is because I want this, I think. *I've always wanted this.*

"Why let this detail be the reason you fail?" he continues. "Because it's against your will? Because it's not something you signed up for? We're athletes. We tackle obstacles. We work hard and continue to work hard no matter what's set in our path. Why is this so different? Why disregard a clear opportunity that's set to *help* you succeed?"

I'm not sure how to answer that.

And he translates my silence to mean I don't want to reply.

He just shakes his head and sighs. "I'm not going to waste my time on a lost cause, Emma. If I invest my time in you, it's to ensure you succeed. I can't push this just to watch you drown in the process. Either work with me or fail on your own. Because you're not the only one in training here. I have dreams, too. And they don't involve having your failure on my conscience."

Colton removes his cap and goggles, dips his head into the water, and then places his palms on the edge of the pool to guide himself up out of the water.

"I put my number in your phone," he says. "Call me when you're ready. Otherwise, best of luck to you, Emma Adrian."

CHAPTER SIX

Colton

I miss Arizona. Not because of the climate or Coach Rogers, but because of the peace it afforded me. In Arizona, I was just Colton the swimmer. Everyone around me was the same, all motivated by similar ideals and goals as I was, and focused on the future.

On Stonewall University grounds, I'm known as Colton Kinsley, son of the famous Clive Kinsley. I also happen to be an Olympian, which makes all the girls giggle and swoon, but they care more about my name than my athletic status. The swimmer part just adds to my physique and physical appeal.

"Hi, Colton," the hostess of Brazenhead Gardens greets with a sigh. "Your mother and brother are this way."

"Thanks," I mutter, already dreading this

meal.

This was one of our traditions every fourth Sunday when I attended Stonewall, and now that I'm back to coach Emma, my mother insisted on restarting the affair.

Connor came up from New York City to meet us.

Mother flew in from Connecticut on the family jet.

My only saving grace is the seven o'clock hour because it means neither of them can stay long after dinner. Connor has work tomorrow, and my mother prefers sleeping in her own bed.

My mother's brown eyes sparkle with delight upon seeing me, her lips curling in greeting. She stands as I approach, and I press my lips to her cheek in the requisite kiss. Then I allow her to hug me while Connor watches with an amused grin.

I flip him off behind her back, but like all mothers, she has an intuition for such things and tsks, "Behave, you two."

Connor smirks.

I roll my eyes.

As though we ever *behave*.

"I've missed you," my mother says as I pull away.

"You just saw me three weeks ago over the holiday break," I reply.

"Yes, three weeks too long," she counters.

I indulge her with a smile and take my place across from my brother. He's dressed in a gray suit today, his cream-colored button-down shirt unfastened at the neck in a display of his version of casual. I chose a black pair of dress pants and paired it with an off-white sweater—which makes me resemble a less classy version of my older brother. We both have the same hair and eyes, but my skin is a little tanner, thanks to my time in Arizona.

Still, we're close enough to pass for twins.

Although, my expression lacks his refined arrogance.

My mother reaches across the table to grab both our hands, her giddiness at having us on either side of her momentarily softening our meeting. She's always been a doting woman, unlike several other females in our social circle.

Cassandra Kinsley preferred to raise her children herself, refusing my father's offer of a nanny countless times. I spent most of my younger years with her, then my life significantly changed at the age of eight when I went off to boarding school in England.

"Where's Emma?" she asks, looking around as though expecting the girl to appear out of thin air. "I assumed you would bring her."

I fight the urge to frown and instead force my features to remain neutral. "She's studying." I have no idea if that's true, and frankly, I don't care.

The infuriating girl is on my last nerve. I watched her during practice this afternoon from the safety of the bleachers above. Afterward, Coach Hawkins asked when I intended to start training her. I told him she wasn't ready yet and left before she even knew I was there.

She would reach out soon enough.

Likely after she receives a certain university email.

I reach out to take a sip of the ice water near my empty plate and hide the vindictive twist of my lips. My mother is studying me, as is my brother, but I don't give anything away. Just set the glass back down and arch a brow. "What? It's not like she's been inducted yet. She's just a recruit."

"An important recruit," my mother corrects.

"Yes, I'm aware of how important she is to you both," I reply flatly. "Except, if that's truly the case, then why was I the one to explain her recruitment status?" The question is for my brother, which I convey by staring straight at him.

His eyes narrow.

And my mother frowns. "You didn't tell her?" she demands of him, her displeasure clear.

If there's one thing I know, it's not to mess with our mum's ideas. And my brother did so by not following through on his task last weekend.

He gives her the same bullshit excuse that he gave me—*work*. Of course, he fails to add the bit about how he feels it's time I earn my position within the Scorpio Society.

"This is an opportunity for you to shine," he said when I called him Friday to chew his ass out. *"Besides, I'm sure she took it just fine."*

She did not take it *just fine*. She took it worse than fine. And now I'm stuck paying for his misstep—a misstep he ensured by failing to tell me that she didn't know.

He absolutely did that on purpose.

Which is why I choose to speak up in front of our mother now.

She bites into him while I watch, my lips curling in an amusement he does not share. He put me in an impossible situation. It only seems fair to return the favor.

Dinner passes in a similar manner with my mother chiding Connor for his less-than-stellar behavior. She continues to say Emma is important to our cause, the perfect addition to the Kinsley Elite.

I play the role of dutiful son as I nod along with everything she says, but by the end, I want to jump off a bridge.

Emma never stood a chance. My mother first noticed the girl at a meet two years ago. Even at seventeen, she was striking, with her thick, dark hair, curvy figure, and long legs. "A prime candidate," my mum called her.

I took one look and shook my head. "Too young for me to say." A bullshit lie because I absolutely noticed her. And now that she's nineteen, I *definitely* noticed her pert tits and tight ass.

Fuck, I'm around beautiful women in swimsuits every day. It takes a lot for me to react.

Emma Adrian makes me react.

Not that I can do anything about it. My role in this test is clear—train her so she passes her test. Then my family will take it from there.

"I want you to bring Emma to our next family night," my mother says as we stand up to leave.

"Is it a family night when Father isn't here?" my brother asks. He's already on Mum's bad side, so he's clearly decided to push it.

However, Cassandra Kinsley isn't a woman to be easily ruffled. She takes hold of his chin, completely undaunted by the fact that he stands almost a foot taller than her five-foot-six height, and pulls his face down so she can look him directly in the eyes. "Your father's presence does not define our family. *We* do."

"Sorry, Mum," he grumbles, doing his best to appear contrite.

He doesn't quite succeed, something our mother confirms by pinching his chin before releasing him. "I'll be sure to let your dad know you miss him."

"Thank you, Mum," he says in that same voice.

I nearly laugh, but I don't want the same thing to happen to my face.

My mother hugs me instead, her lips at my ear. "Do your best to tame her, Colton. You know how much our family will expect from her."

My desire to laugh disappears beneath a wave of resentment. I do my best to hide it from my expression as she releases me. "Of course, Mum."

She kisses my cheek, and I do the same to hers.

Connor reaches for my hand. I bat it away and hug him. We have our differences, but we're still close despite our five-year age gap.

"Call me if you need advice," he says softly.

"I could have used some advice Friday before I royally pissed off the family recruit," I counter.

He shrugs. "Maybe it'll put some hair on your chest."

I roll my eyes at the old jibe. He knows perfectly well that I shave for swimming. And he's always poked fun at me for it. "I hate you."

"I love you, too," he jokes, winking as he pulls away.

My mother beams at us, entertained by our usual banter. Then her eyes take on a teary gleam, and I sigh. She hates goodbyes. "We'll see you in four weeks," I promise her.

"I know," she whispers. She reaches for our hands once more and gives them a squeeze. "Take me to the airport," she tells Connor as she releases me but holds on to him.

He gives me a knowing look—Mum only requests alone time when she has a lecture on her mind.

I silently wish him luck, bid them goodbye, and run away before she decides I need to be involved in whatever she wants to say.

If there's one thing I know about my family, it's to escape when given the chance.

I would plan to teach Emma the same thing, but she'll never have the opportunity to flee. She's been chosen. Now I just need her to accept it.

And I have a pretty good idea on how to do that.

She doesn't want me around? Then I'll leave and give her some time to think it over. Then we'll see how she feels after a few weeks on her own with this looming death sentence hanging over her head.

I'll be waiting for your call, I think as I slide into the driver's seat of my favorite car. *Until then, good luck, little pledge.*

CHAPTER SEVEN

Emma

What the hell? The email in my inbox has me frowning and cursing out loud.

"Colton." It comes out on a snarl of sound, my teeth gnawing together as I study my *revised* schedule. It's all the same classes, but my afternoon course has been bumped up by ninety minutes and moved to a location that's a block away from the aquatics center.

This is definitely not a coincidence.

I shove my laptop into my bag with my books and decide to properly deal with him later.

It's been two days since we last spoke, but I sensed him at practice yesterday and this morning. He's like a presence that taunts my conscience. I didn't actually see him, but I *felt* him.

I check Rylie's room on my way out, noting

her fully made bed. My lips twist to the side. I haven't heard from her other than a short text to tell me she's okay. Her room suggests she hasn't been home since Friday, but that's more of an instinct than a deduction. She's not the messy sort, so it's hard to say when she was last here.

Rylie's self-sufficient, I remind myself as I lock up our dorm room. *If she says she's okay, then she's okay*.

I'm just feeling off because of everything with Colton and the events from Friday night.

And my altered schedule.

As well as Colton's words from Saturday. His statements haunt my every step on my way to the campus cafeteria for breakfast—which feels more like lunch since I've been awake for five hours and already participated in morning practice.

His comments continue to swim through my thoughts during my economics course.

They follow me to lunch.

And they stay with me for my newly rescheduled statistics course.

As a statistics major, I should be able to shove Colton's voice to the back of my thoughts, but his words are like a wave in my thoughts, rolling on repeat and demanding I listen.

I know he's right; he's offered me the experience of a lifetime. I also accepted my Stonewall scholarship because of him—because

I wanted to be close to him, to learn from him, to swim like him.

He essentially gave me everything I wanted. Just with the small, minor detail that my life is the price I'll pay if I screw this up.

As if there isn't enough pressure to perform at this level, he added a potential death sentence to it.

I tried searching for the Scorpio Society online yesterday. Nothing came back. And given what he told me, I probably set off some sort of alarm with my research.

I kept waiting for him to call and tell me to cut it out.

But nothing.

Silence.

He just… let me be.

Which suggests he meant what he said. *"Call me when you're ready. Otherwise, best of luck to you, Emma Adrian."*

I shiver as I recall his final statement.

Professor Neilson dismisses class soon after, not once remarking on the change of location or time. Perhaps she felt the email from the school was enough to explain the oddity of having a course moved.

I don't stick around to ask questions.

Instead, I gather up my stuff and head back to my dorm room to drop off my bag. Since I now have ninety minutes to spare, it's an easy thing to do.

Rylie is in the living room with a bag when I enter, her expression tainting with surprise at seeing me. "Hey, Em," she greets as though we didn't part on strange terms Friday night.

"You're okay," I say, more for myself than for her. *See. She's okay.* Some of the weight I've been carrying around all day leaves my shoulders, and I breathe a little easier.

Until Colton's words reverberate in my head for the millionth time.

Buzz off, I think, trying futilely to drown out his voice.

"Uh, yeah, I'm okay." She steps closer and lowers her voice. "But I have *Scorpio* stuff to do."

My eyes widen. "Scorpio?" It comes out on a squeak, and she shushes me.

"I don't know how much we're allowed to say, you know? But Roman told me you're a recruit, too. So I guess… I guess we both have things to do right now, yeah?"

I gape at her. "You know about all this? What they want me to do?"

She shakes her head. "No, and don't tell me. It's not my place to know. Just like I can't share my test with you. But maybe once we're initiated…?" She shrugs as if to say, *We'll see*.

"Shit. This is really happening, isn't it?" I can't help the note of wonder in my tone. I spent the last few days questioning my sanity and waiting to wake up from this bizarre dream. But Rylie being a recruit, too, just makes it that much more *real*.

Rylie's lips quirk into a wry smile. "Yeah, it's definitely happening. But if you think you're imagining it, we can have a shrink session later."

I roll my eyes. "Cute. Very cute."

Rylie grins. "I know." A beat passes and her amusement begins to die. "I… need to stay with Roman for a bit. Are you going to be staying with Colton?"

I snort. "Not if I can help it."

"So it's going well, then?"

"If you mean me wanting to kill him? Then, yes, very well."

Her expression sobers a bit. "He's one of the Elders' sons. From what I understand, that's a pretty big deal. So I would be careful about pissing him off."

"Too late for that," I mutter.

Concern etches into her features. "Seriously, Em. This… this is a big deal. I don't know all the details yet, but this society is crazy connected." She glances around, her brow furrowing. "And they probably bugged our room, so I hope talking about this doesn't get us in trouble."

"You think it'll get us in trouble?"

"I think it's an intense organization that takes secrecy very seriously." There's no sign of sarcasm in her features, her concern palpable. "I really should go. I don't want to risk either of our statuses. Just... take care of yourself, okay? And if you pissed off Colton, then apologize."

I bite my lip. "That may be hard to do."

"Try," she insisted, reaching out to wrap her slender arms around my shoulders. "Whatever they want you to do, do it."

Solemn words.

Ones I hesitate to repeat back to her.

Because I'm not sure I'm in this the way she is, at least not yet.

So I whisper, "I'll try."

"Don't try; *do*," she replies. "Isn't that what you always say about swimming?"

She has no idea how pertinent that is to my situation. "Yes," I admit. "I do."

"You *do*," she agrees. "This isn't any different." She squeezes my shoulder before releasing me. "I'll have my phone. Use my number if you need me. I'll... I'll do my best to help."

I nod. Because we both know there's nothing she can do to help me, just as I can't help her.

The Scorpio Society tapped both of us, I marvel as she leaves. *What are the odds?* Given the student population numbers, I suspect those odds are quite low.

Or maybe that's why we're roommates. Did the Scorpio Society organize that, too? If they can redo my schedule without so much as a blink, then it seems quite possible that our living situation was prearranged as well.

I stare down at the floor for an unknown length of time. Then I glance around my quarters and wonder if Rylie's right about it being bugged.

The thought gives me chills.

I pull out my phone and consider texting to ask him.

No, I decide. *I'll ask him at practice instead.*

Because then I can read his facial expression.

With a nod, I prepare for practice and head to the natatorium, ready to talk to Colton.

Who doesn't show up for practice.

Or magically appear afterward either.

It's almost like he knew, which only proves to make me more paranoid.

When he doesn't show up for practice all week, I start to wonder what's happening. Then I overhear Lanie telling Jesi that Colton's gone back to Arizona to resume training with Coach Rogers. "I guess he didn't feel we were good enough to swim with," she concludes sourly.

"Not us, but the men's team," Jesi says. "This"—she gestures down her long, streamlined sprinter body—"could never keep up with the likes of him." She glances at me. "The only one who could somewhat give him a challenge is you, Em."

I wince, her words striking home. "Well, I guess he feels otherwise." And I only have myself to blame for it. Not that I can explain my predicament to anyone.

Because I'm on my own, I realize, his words piercing my mind once more.

"Best of luck to you, Emma Adrian."

Shit.

I should have apologized. Or reached out to say I was ready.

But I haven't felt ready at all.

Not until right now.

When it's already too late.

CHAPTER EIGHT

Emma

Three weeks and two swim meets later, and nothing from Colton.

I finally gave in and texted him four days ago. No reply.

I'm interpreting that to mean that he's given up on me entirely and I'm on my own. Part of me is terrified. The other part is pissed. He gave me no time to accept this fate, no time to acknowledge all this insanity with the Scorpio Society, and no time to get used to the idea of working with him.

My jaw clenches as I warm up for my next event.

Our team is at an away meet tonight, over two hundred miles from Stonewall University. So we'll be staying at a hotel after. I'm not looking forward to it because I'm rooming with Jesi and

Lanie, and they've already expressed interest in going out to explore campus nightlife. It's a Friday; I get it. But all I really want to do is pass out.

Blowing out a breath, I pull myself out of the warm-up side of the pool and grab my towel. A few other swimmers glance at me along the way. I smile—or try to, anyway. My mind is frazzled, thanks to a certain Olympian.

I'll text him again after the meet, I decide. *Maybe I'll grovel a little.*

If I can.

I already sent him an apology with my *I'm ready* text. But maybe he wants a more detailed expression of regret. Because apparently *I'm sorry* isn't good enough.

With a shake of my head, I clear it and focus on the ten lanes sprawled out before me. It's a fifty-meter pool with a bulkhead in the middle dividing the racing section from the warm-up section.

Not a bad setup.

But I really don't like the way bulkheads feel under my feet. They always seem to bounce. It's why I prefer long course swimming, which, thankfully, is used for the Olympics.

Colton wants me to focus on my turns.

Well, there are far fewer turns in long course events because it's fifty meters instead of twenty-five yards.

Thank the heavens for that.

Sadly, it won't help me much tonight.

A hundred-meter backstroke has three flip turns. This is my third-best event behind the butterfly and individual medley, marking it as my most obvious choice for Olympic competition. The problem is, I'm closer to a tenth or eleventh ranking nationally.

Freestyle is the other event I'm considering.

It's something I could ask Colton, but he's not here.

Because I chased him off.

Shut up and focus, I tell myself, studying the lanes again. It's my pre-race ritual to envision myself in the water, counting my strokes, practicing my turns, and considering my breaths. Backstroke is easier on the last point since my face will be above water the whole time, but this event is all about pacing.

I close my eyes, losing myself to the mood of the natatorium, the water, the pool, the race. I roll my neck, loosen my arms, and bend to stretch my legs. It's not a big meet, just against a single team, and I know who their best swimmers are.

No competition.

But that's fine because I prefer to compete with myself.

If I stand any chance of qualifying for the Olympics in this event, then I need to start shaving off time. It's mid-season, I'm not tapered, and I'm exhausted, but that can't stop me from trying.

My event is next on deck.

I place my towel on a chair, check my cap, and adjust my goggles. The thing I like best about backstroke is I get to feel the water before the race begins. It's the only event that has a swimmer jump in first to do a start off the handlebars of the block.

A shiver trickles over my skin, the air cool, but not too cold.

I shake out my arms again, my eyes on the water as the race before mine completes. I nod to my teammate, congratulating the win without looking at the times. It's irrelevant to me and my impending sprint.

Because that's what a one hundred backstroke is—a sprint.

I prefer the two hundred because it allows me to catch my pace. Maybe I'll pick that event for competition at the trials.

Shoving the future from my mind, I focus on the present as the official blows his whistle to signal our heat to enter.

I jump into the water, my feet coming nowhere near the bottom. It's a deep pool, which makes it cold and perfect for competition.

With a final roll of my neck, I grab the bars above me and place my feet just below the water's surface.

A hush falls through the natatorium, the small audience aware of the requirement for silence.

"Take your mark," the official says.

Beep.

I shove off the wall into a back arch, my arms flying above my head in a backward dive to streamline my entry.

Kick. Kick. Kick.

This is my strength—the underwater butterfly kick. I surface just before the disqualification marker—there's only so much underwater swimming allowed—and I begin counting my strokes.

I'm at the first wall in a flash, dipping and spinning and pushing with all my might.

Kick. Kick. Kick.

Again.

The water moves beneath my power, my stroke cutting through the lane at a beautiful speed I feel all the way to my toes.

Flags. Count. Flip. Push. Kick. Kick. Kick.

Two laps to go.

This is where sprinters lose speed and I pick up my pace.

Third wall comes and goes in a splash.

And I'm on the final leg, propelling myself through the water in the way I was born to do.

Flags. Count. Dip back. Palm meets wall.

My body burns with adrenaline, my breath

choking out of me as the exhilaration of the sprint catches up with me. And I look up at the board to see my time.

Not my placing in the race, because I don't care about that right now—and I already know I won since the others are finishing in my peripheral vision. But it's the time that counts.

And it's not the time I want.

It's almost a second off my personal best.

Damn.

I want to blame the pool. I want to blame my exhausted, un-tapered state. I want to blame my layered suit.

But I know the truth.

Mind over matter.

I psyched myself out before I even began.

With a mental sigh, I pull myself out of the water. Several teammates clap me on the back saying, "Great swim."

I smile with a "Thanks."

The rest of the evening is a blur. I try to give my all in the relay but add time there, too. And I just feel generally off.

So when Jesi and Lanie ask me to go out with them, I accept.

Because what do I have to lose at this point? Tomorrow will be a driving day on the bus. No practice. And I may die in June.

Only live once, I decide.

Jesi lends me one of her dresses because I

only packed yoga pants and sweatshirts. "Always come prepared," she says as she lays out five different outfits across the hotel bed for me to choose from.

Crazy girl, I think, not for the first time. She picks the cute purple halter dress that pretty much paints a "Pay attention to me" sign across her breasts.

I go for the black one because it matches my mood.

It hits me midthigh, which is truly inappropriate for the weather outside. But she gives me a matching sweater to pair on top. Then she hands me her knee-high boots. They're about a size too small for my feet, but I make do. The heels are going to kill me by the end of the night, though.

After a parade of makeup and hair products, we're ready to go, and Jesi leads the way to some party one of the girls on the other team told her about after the meet.

I don't overthink it; I just follow.

And I leave my phone behind.

CHAPTER NINE

Colton

Little brat, I think as Emma slips from the hotel with two other swimmers from the team.

After her display in the pool this evening, I half expected her to be back in her room, analyzing every mistake she made.

But no.

She's wandering out into the night with her friends, dressed in a sinfully short dress and fuck-me heels.

I resist the urge to growl and instead dial one of my buddies on the local university team. One thing I love about this sport is knowing swimmers around the world.

"Colton," Craig drawls after the second ring. "I thought I saw you lurking in the stands. Surprised to see you with the women's team, though. I'd expect you at the men's meet. You know, to watch your competition and all."

I snort. "What competition? And I wasn't lurking. I was sitting." I just happened to be near the back and out of Emma's view. Not that she even bothered to look. Her focus on the meet was about the only thing she did right tonight. "Why didn't you come say hi?"

"I was busy psyching up Rach."

"Ah." I've met his girlfriend once or twice. Decent sprinter. But not on the Olympic radar. "She swim well tonight?" It's only polite to ask. Even more polite to know the answer myself, but my focus was on Emma all night.

"She did all right. That Emma chick kicked her ass in the backstroke, though."

I frown. *Rachel was in that race?* "Oh." I'm not sure what else to say other than, "Yeah, Emma's got some talent."

"She's a fucking dolphin."

I smirk. "Definitely that." Her legs are all power and grace. "Anyway, I was wondering what parties are happening on campus tonight. I'm bored."

"Colton Kinsley attend a party?" A shuffling sound comes through the line. "Sorry, I was checking the caller ID."

"I just want to get some fresh air."

"Are you high on chlorine?"

I roll my eyes at the jibe. Yeah, I have a

reputation for preferring to sleep over attending parties. It's the price I pay for greatness. "Stop fucking with me and give me the details."

He chuckles and gives me what I'm looking for.

"Thanks," I say.

"See you there?"

"Maybe," I reply vaguely. Because I don't necessarily intend to be *seen*.

That's been my mode for the last few weeks, practicing on my own in my in-home pool and spending countless hours in my own exercise room afterward.

Emma's text the other night gave me a tad of hope, which is why I traveled out here to watch her meet.

Her performance in the water left a lot to be desired. Oh, she won. Fuck, she killed her competition. But that's not what matters. Her strokes were off. Her walls were crap. And her headspace was all wrong.

We have a lot of work to do.

And she's off to party.

"Tease," Craig accuses. "If I tell Rach you're coming, she'll tell the whole women's team. And if you don't show, they'll be devastated."

"Then don't tell anyone anything," I suggest.

He sighs. "Always secretive and unpredictable."

"It keeps life interesting," I reply.

We hang up a minute later, and I head outside just as Emma disappears into a car. One of the girls must have called for a ride. Great. Now Emma's trusting strangers to drive her around.

I suppose it's normal to call a designated driver for the night. But Emma Adrian isn't supposed to be normal. And it's time she realizes that.

I don't call for a ride of my own; I drive. Because I don't plan on having anything to drink.

Parking on campus isn't ideal, but I find a place a few blocks off frat row and head toward the address Craig gave me.

It's a bit of a walk, but once I'm on the right street, it doesn't take long for me to find the party. There have to be at least a hundred people on the lawn and inside the ornate mansion. It reminds me of Stonewall a little, only the colors are black and blue instead of crimson and gold.

Minton University is a small private school with only fifteen thousand students. It's elite and expensive and one of Stonewall's rivals in the pool.

The Stonewall Sinners women's team won tonight.

But no one seems to care as they socialize and enjoy each other's company inside.

I spy Emma laughing with some football player—an estimate due to his bulky size—as he tries to show her how to play beer pong out on the wraparound porch.

It's an activity she should absolutely not be engaging in.

She's underage and in the middle of training, and I made the rules very clear. But here she is breaking a handful of them with a smile on her pretty face.

It makes me want to pull her over my knee and give her a few slaps on the ass for being disobedient.

And that thought makes me hard as a damn rock.

This girl is going to be the fucking death of me.

She shakes her head when the football dude tries to encourage her to play. He frowns. She gives him some sort of excuse and leaves him at the table staring after her with puppy dog eyes.

I snort, amused by his expression, and pursue my little pledge into the crowded house.

It becomes clear after a few minutes that she's looking for someone, probably the girls she arrived with. But after a few minutes, her brow crinkles and she bites her lip. It's an adorable look of confusion mingled with concern.

And I'm about to exacerbate it by a million.

I circle around behind her, standing between her back and the wall, and capture her hips with my hands. She jolts and tries to twist away, but I yank her backward and into the shadows of the dimly lit living area.

"Not only is it after ten, but I do believe this is a party, darling pledge," I say against her ear. "Good thing you turned down the alcohol. That would have been three broken rules. And I really hope you brought protection, or that's a potential fourth mark on your record. All in one night."

"Colton," she says, frozen against me.

"Emma." I twirl her in my arms so I can stare into her beautiful, startled eyes. "What am I going to do with you?"

CHAPTER TEN

Emma

"What are you doing here?" I breathe, the words barely processing over the harsh bass of the music resounding through the house.

Colton seems to hear me just fine, as he shrugs casually while saying, "I watched the meet earlier. Came out tonight to get laid, but imagine my surprise when I saw you dressed like a vixen inside."

He pulls me close until my breasts are smashed up against his chest. The fabric of my dress is so thin that I can almost feel the fibers of his black sweater brushing my skin.

"Now, I'm curious," he drawls. "Where did you hide your protection in this dress?"

I blink at him. "Wh-what?"

"Protection," he enunciates. Whatever he

sees on my face causes him to tsk. "That's four rules, then. I'm very disappointed."

I shake my head, trying to clear my thoughts. *What the heck does protection....?* My eyes widen. "Oh, no. No, no. I wasn't... You're the one who's here to get laid, not me." It comes out louder than I anticipated, causing a few people around us to glance over.

Colton smirks and uses his hands on my hips to pull me deeper into the hallway where it's a little quieter. "Sweetheart, in a dress like this, you're looking to get laid."

I nearly growl at him. "So you're one of those guys? Accusing a girl of asking for it because of the way she's dressed?"

He rolls his eyes. "That's not what I meant at all."

"That's the way it sounded."

"You're deflecting because of the protection issue."

"No, I'm deflecting because I should be allowed to wear whatever the hell I want with no expectations." And I'm totally ignoring the "protection issue" because I don't want to talk about it with him. "It's none of your business what I do."

"Oh, little pledge, on that, we strongly disagree. Your body is your trophy. Poison it, and you'll fail the test. That's why I told you to always bring protection. Unless you're on the pill? But even then, that's not going to protect you from diseases."

"I cannot believe you are lecturing me on this."

"And I can't believe I have to lecture you on it," he counters, his grip tightening on my hips. "You have to protect yourself, Emma. That means no partying. No illegal substances, which includes alcohol as an underage student at a party. And no fucking without protection."

"Oh my God!" I'm ready to kill him. "I did not come here to get laid!" I've given up caring who can hear me. Although, this little nook he's found feels oddly private for such a large party.

But whatever.

This is ridiculous.

"I've only had sex once," I continue, furious. "And the experience wasn't worth a repeat. So when I say I'm not here for a *fuck*, I mean it."

He gapes at me like this is shocking information. "Only once?"

"Seriously? That's all you heard from my statement?" I roll my eyes. "Heath Baxter at nationals last summer. Well, after the last day of the meet." I shrug. "I figured I should try it once, and I immediately regretted it. So trust me, I don't want to do it again. Satisfied?"

"Not at all. Why did you regret it?" He sounds suspicious. "Did he force you?"

I snort. "No. It was just…" I trail off, trying

to figure out how to describe it. Then I realize that I don't owe him a damn thing, let alone an explanation. "You know what? Forget I mentioned it. I don't even know why I told you. The point is, *I'm fine*. And I didn't break a rule, because I didn't intend on... you know."

"Fucking," he says.

"That," I mutter. "Can we not talk about this anymore?" I'm not even sure how our conversation devolved into this. He accused me of wanting to hook up. I told him I didn't. And yeah. This... this is... it's something else.

And does he really need to hold me this close? It's frying brain cells.

"If I find out he forced you—"

"He didn't," I interject. "On God's green earth, you're gonna make me say this, aren't you? It sucked, and I never want to do it again. Therefore, your *rule* does not apply to me. Got it?" My cheeks are burning from the embarrassment of having this conversation with him, which only irritates me more. "And even if it did, I know how to use a damn condom."

But if he asks me to demonstrate, I'm going to make him eat the rubber instead.

His lips curl like he knows that's what I'm thinking. Or maybe it's my words. I don't really care. This conversation went in a direction I never anticipated, and now I'm warm and prickly all over, and I'm not a fan.

Who is he to make all these rules, anyway?

"Do you have a condom?" I ask him bluntly. "Since you're such a fan of the *rules*, I assume they apply to you as well?"

"I always have one in my wallet," he replies. "It's a gentleman's responsibility to be prepared."

I huff a laugh. "Gentleman. Right. You don't even know the meaning of the term."

His eyebrows lift. "Is that an insult?"

"Probably," I admit, daring him to chastise me.

Then another thought smacks me in the head as the music changes to a new tune.

"Wait, why are you allowed to party and I'm not?" I demand.

"Because I'm legally allowed to drink alcohol," he says without missing a beat. Then his gaze narrows. "What would happen if cops busted this party right now? You and I both know how important image is in our sport."

His words strike home, sending a shock through my system.

He has a point.

It wouldn't matter that I didn't have a drink in my hand. I'm underage and surrounded by intoxicated students. Guilty by association.

Swimmers don't exactly attract a great deal of media attention, but we're strongly judged within our sport.

And being a party girl isn't the reputation I

want.

Colton's hands slide to my lower back as he begins to sway with me to the beat of the music. I'm not sure if he's doing it to try to loosen my suddenly stiff stance or if it's something he does without realizing it.

"Y-you're right," I stammer, hating the weakness in my tone. And hating even more that I'm agreeing with him out loud. Especially after everything he just yanked out of me through an incredibly awkward conversation. "But I didn't drink," I add.

"I know," he replies, his palm slipping up my back to hold me even closer as his lips go to my ear. "I was watching you."

I shiver, his breath hot against my skin. "Oh," I whisper.

His body moves against mine, forcing me to break out of my stiff state. "That's better," he says. "People were beginning to stare."

With my back to the entrance of the hallway, I can't see anyone but Colton.

But at least now I know why he's dancing with me. I try to ignore the way it feels to be pressed up against him and instead focus on his earlier statements. "You watched the meet?" My voice is a little steadier now, my anxiety melting into something else entirely.

Something darker.

Needier.

A distracting element, one I try not to recognize.

However, it's difficult not to notice Colton's heat... or his masculine form... or his strong, knowing grip.

"I did," he murmurs, his lips still touching my ear. "Your focus was admirable. The rest was not."

I grunt. "I sucked."

He lifts his mouth away from my ear to stare down at me. "Yeah, you did."

I merely nod. It's futile to belabor the point or fret over it. "I need to train harder."

"You do."

"And I need to pick two more events," I continue.

"Yes," he agrees.

I nod again. "I don't want to be here." It's an admission that I don't mean to make, but it's true nonetheless. It's also a statement that encompasses so many things.

I don't want to be in this situation with the Scorpio Society.

I don't want to be at this lower level of swimming when I know I can accomplish more.

And I don't want to be at this party.

"I know," Colton says, his lips ghosting over my cheek on the way to my ear. "Follow me outside, and I'll take you back to the hotel."

I'm too tired to argue with him. Too

emotionally beat to consider another alternative. I just do what he says—or I try to, anyway. But he's held up near the door by Craig Taylor. I've never met him. However, I know of him and his ability in the pool. He's a backstroker. Tall, lanky, lean muscle.

He swipes his fingers through his thick blond hair as he grins at Colton. "I can't believe you actually came, Kinsley. This has to be a momentous occasion of some kind." Then his green eyes land on me, and understanding graces his features. "Ah, I see."

Colton gives him a look. "Trust me, it's not like that at all. She's nineteen and a freshman. I'm just mentoring."

Well, he doesn't need to sound so disgusted by the idea of it being something else.

But whatever.

The feeling's mutual.

I totally did not have a reaction to him dancing close to me seconds ago. Like, none at all. Not even a little tingle.

My lips threaten to curl down.

Lying, especially to myself, was never my strong suit.

"Uh-huh," Craig says, looking between us.

Colton just shakes his head. "I'll catch you another time, man. Emma's out after curfew."

Part of me wants to snap at him for treating me like a child. The other part of me notices Jesi and Lanie watching nearby with slacked jaws, and I decide I don't want to cause more of a scene. "I'll see you both back at the hotel."

"No, she'll see you in the pool on Monday," he corrects. "We have some training to do this weekend. I'll drive her back myself."

"There's the Colton I know and hate," Craig drawls. "Always focused on the pool."

"It's why I win," Colton returns with a grin.

Craig just laughs and shrugs. "Yeah, yeah." He's a decent swimmer, but not at the Olympic level like Colton. He probably could be if he tried a little harder. But given the beer in his hand and his lazy grin now, I can see that's just not who he is. Not everyone wants this.

Because not everyone has the drive like Colton and I do.

I allow him to lead me away from the party for that reason and that reason alone.

It's time I take charge of my future and do what I came here to do—*win*.

"All right, Coach Colton," I say as he opens the door to his car a few blocks away from the party. "Let's see what you've got."

He grins. "Game on."

"Game on," I repeat.

Because I want this. I want to go to the Olympics. I want to be the best of the best.

And most importantly, I want to live.

Thank you for reading Colton's Secret. The story continues with Colton's Legacy.

Colton's Legacy
Kinsley Elite Duet Part I

Colton Kinsley is a swimming god.
He's also my coach, my captor, and my eventual
executioner.
Unless I pass my trials.

The Kinsley family is part of an old secret
organization born of wealth and prestige.
The Scorpio Society.
His father is an Elder.
And his mother picked me as their pledge for
this semester's initiate class.

Qualify for five individual Olympic events.
That's my task.
With Colton as my guide.

I now have five months to train.
Five months to master my strokes.
Five months to prepare for the trial of a
lifetime.
If I fail, I die.

Swimming saves lives.
But am I good enough for it to save mine?

ABOUT A.C. KRAMER

USA Today Bestselling Author A.C. Kramer is the New Adult & Contemporary Romance pseudonym for Lexi C. Foss. New Adult Romance is her guilty pleasure, coffee is her addiction, and swimming is her escape.

For details about current and future works, check out her website below:

https://www.authorackramer.com/